PUFFIN BOOKS

The Great Smile Robbery

Emerson has a nice smile. In fact, he has a cupboard full of smiles – warmhearted ones, cheeky ones, shy ones, sad ones, straightforward 'how do you do' ones, and just a few he's made up himself. So when a nationwide competition is announced to find the Best Smile in the World, Emerson should certainly be in with a chance.

Unfortunately, Billy Bogie, Mrs Wobblebottom, Nick O'Teen, King Pong and the rest of the villainous Stinker Gang have dastardly plans for winning the competition themselves, and poor Emerson is soon in desperate trouble!

How Emerson outwits the Stinkers and survives a day of robberies, amazing bus journeys and other exciting happenings makes hilarious reading. With his customary verve and vitality (and not a little silliness), Roger McGough has written a very funny book which will delight young readers.

Roger McGough was born in Liverpool and made a name for himself there with his poems and his efforts to popularize poetry. He has written many books of poetry and a number of plays. He has frequently appeared on television and gives amusing and successful readings from his work in schools and universities, and at Arts Festivals in Britain, America and Europe.

D0755836

Some other books by Roger McGough

SKY IN THE PIE
YOU TELL ME (with Michael Rosen)
STRICTLY PRIVATE: an anthology of poetry
THE STOWAWAYS

The Great Smile Robbery
by Roger McGough

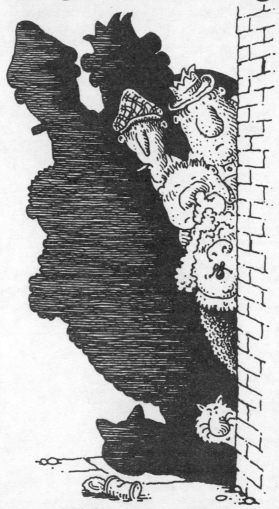

Illustrated by Tony Blundell
PUFFIN BOOKS

This one is for Tom

PUFFIN BOOKS

Published by the Penguin Group
27 Wrights Lane, London W8 5TZ, England
Viking Penguin Inc., 40 West 23rd Street, New York, New York 10010, USA
Penguin Books Australia Ltd, Ringwood, Victoria, Australia
Penguin Books Canada Ltd, 2801 John Street, Markham, Ontario, Canada L3R 1B4
Penguin Books (NZ) Ltd, 182–190 Wairau Road, Auckland 10, New Zealand

Penguin Books Ltd, Registered Offices: Harmondsworth, Middlesex, England

First published by Kestrel Books 1982
Published in Puffin Books 1984
10 9 8 7 6 5

Copyright © Roger McGough, 1982
Illustrations copyright © Tony Blundell, 1982
All rights reserved

Made and printed in Great Britain by
Richard Clay Ltd, Bungay, Suffolk

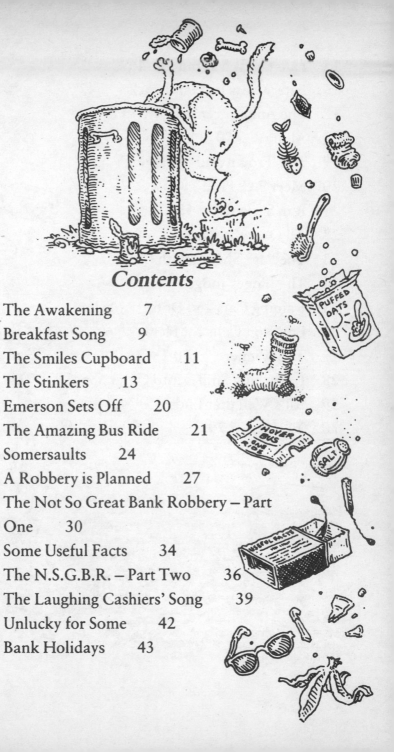

Contents

1 The Awakening

Emerson was in the habit, like most of us, of waking up every morning. Thursday was no exception. It was the first morning of spring 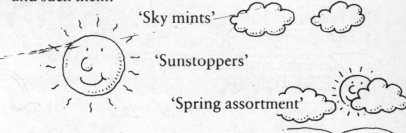 the cleanest day of the year. The air so crisp and clear you could snap bits off and suck them:

'Sky mints'

'Sunstoppers'

'Spring assortment'

Emerson opened the window and took a deep breath. Then another. Feeling wonderfully refreshed, he put the breaths back and closed the window.

He brushed his teeth under and over. Washed his face inside and out. Combed his hair through and through until there were no knots. Not any. Not a knot whatsoever on his whatnot.

And of course, being the hero of this story, he did all these things without being told.

(So be warned – if you do everything right away without being asked, and always say 'please' and 'thank you' – you might end up as a character in a story. And it's no fun, believe me, spending half your life stuck inside a closed book on a dusty shelf in a dark room.)

Anyway, back to the story . . .

2 Breakfast Song

It was time for breakfast and getting it ready was a
ritual that Emerson enjoyed every morning come hail,
rain or puffed wheat.

So, as he set the table
    and filled the milkjug
    and poured out the cereal
    and warmed the teapot
    and buttered the toast,
He sang the first song of the day:

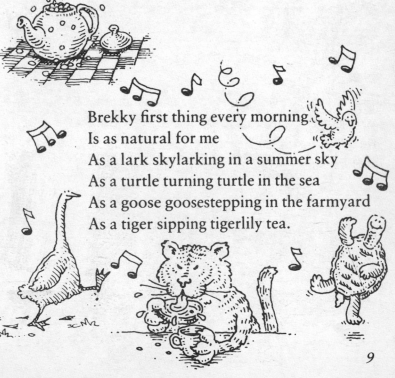

Brekky first thing every morning
Is as natural for me
As a lark skylarking in a summer sky
As a turtle turning turtle in the sea
As a goose goosestepping in the farmyard
As a tiger sipping tigerlily tea.

9

Brekky first thing every morning
Is as natural each day
As a pussy pussyfooting pussy willow
As an eager beaver beavering away
As an eagle eagle-eyeing legal beagles
As a possum playing possum in the hay.

3 The Smiles Cupboard

When the breakfast things had been thanked, washed and put back to sleep in the drawer marked: 'Breakfast Things', Emerson had come to the most important part of the day – choosing what to wear.

Now I don't mean clothes. As long as they were clean, he didn't really care what clothes he wore.

But what was important was to choose the right smile.

Emerson owned lots. He had a cupboard full:

'warmhearted ones'
'cheeky ones'
straightforward 'how do you do?' ones
'shy ones'
'sad ones'

And even a few he'd made up himself. So each morning, before going out to greet the world, he would stand in front of the mirror and try on his smiles.

4   The Stinkers

Most people, of course, who lived in Emerson's neck of the town, loved to meet him walking down the road. His cheerful smiles would make them feel warm all over (warm all under as well).

But there was one gang who lived at the bottom of the street who hated smiles. They were known as the 'Stinkers'. Yes. STINKERS.

They stunk.

They stinked.

If they stood in fields they frightened away the birds. They only had to walk past for babies to start crying, dogs whine and flowers wither. Fearful monsters kept away from Emerson's street after dark.

Now meet the Stinkers . . .

(if you dare)

Billy Bogie:

who picked his nose for hours and hours,
snarled, sneered and spat at flowers.

Mrs Wobblebottom:

who ate more than a Lady should,
fat as a factory, dark as a wood.

Nick O'Teen:

who smoked and smoked and liked to boast
(his insides hot as burning toast).

Sourpuss:

the fleabiting cat who lived in a bin,
ate pickled mice and drank stale gin.

King Pong:

who never washed between his toes
so cabbages grew there in neat little rows.

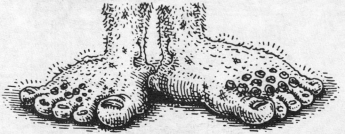

I bet you're glad *you* don't live in Emerson's street.

5 Emerson Sets Off

'I know what I'll do today,' thought Emerson (knowing what he would do). 'I shall take a ride into town on one of the Corporation's amazing new buses. While I am there I will do some shopping, meet my friends for tea, take my books back to the library and get back here in time for page 59.'

So, having selected a springy sort of smile to suit the day, he set off without further adieu.

And, having nobody interesting to watch anymore, the four walls of his house stared dully at each other across the empty rooms.

6 The Amazing Bus Ride

Emerson joined the queue at the corner of Corner Street and Close Encounters of the Third Kind Avenue, and within minutes one of the Corporation's amazing new buses stopped to pick everybody up.

It was a hoverbus, with a rocket booster that enabled it to leap more than thirty feet into the air. So it could leapfrog over lorries, and hurdle over bridges. It was the craziest ride in town.

And when the driver was in a particularly good mood (and today he certainly was, because it was payday) he could even make the bus turn somersaults (all the passengers were strapped in, so it was *quite* safe). 'Hang on everybody,' he yelled, as they

approached the top of Barnacle Hill, 'we're going to try for a double somersault.' Everybody gasped, including Emerson, who couldn't even spell somersault, never mind do one. And this was to be a *double* – phew! He was agosh with excitement.

23

7 Somersaults

The bus seemed to pause (for what seemed like an instant) at the top of the hill and take a deep breath, like a ski-jumper about to begin his lightning descent.

And down it went. W-H-O-O-S-H

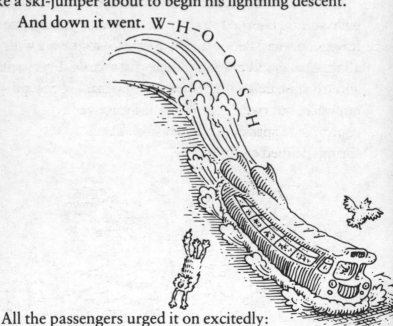

All the passengers urged it on excitedly:

'Come on number 43,' they chanted.

'Faster. Faster.'

Even Mrs Crumble who, at eighty-six, might have been forgiven for hiding under her seat, closing her eyes and saying her prayers, was waving her stick with the excitement of a five-year-old and yelling out in a wrinkled voice:

'You can do it, 43. You can do it.'

The bus reached the foot of the hill at a tremendous pace and then jerked sharply up a small, steep incline. It was a perfect take-off. The bus took to the air with all the speed and grace of a baby Concorde. Everyone aboard squealed with delight as they spun in the air – not once, but twice. Looping the loop over a countryside spread out on all sides like a spring-cleaned counterpane.

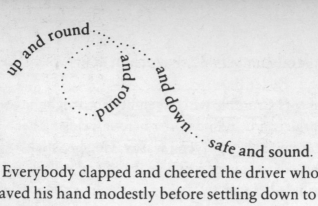

up and round ·····

·····and down·····

and round

·····and down·····

·····safe and sound.

Everybody clapped and cheered the driver who waved his hand modestly before settling down to continue the journey in the old old-fashioned way.

Bus business was soon back to normal.

'Fares please,' said the conductor.

'No they don't,' thought Emerson, fumbling for his change.

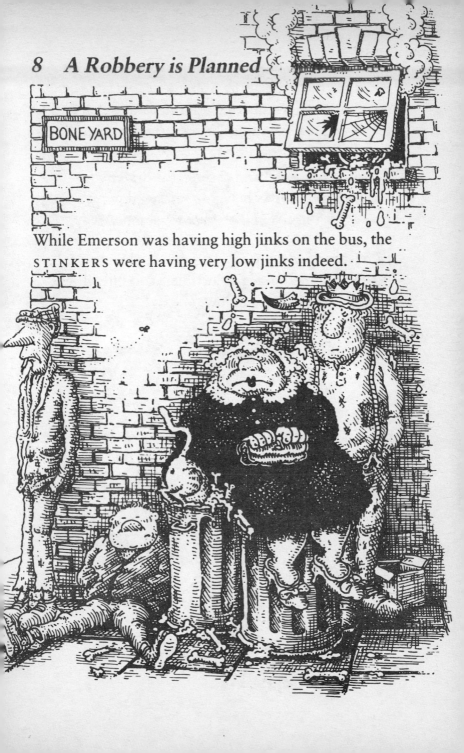

8 A Robbery is Planned

BONE YARD

While Emerson was having high jinks on the bus, the STINKERS were having very low jinks indeed.

Bored as usual, they were lounging around in an alleyway at the back of the Abbatoir. It was one of their favourite places because of the sickly smell and the sticky squeals of things being turned into lamb chops, bacon and roast beef.

'What shall we do today?' meeyawned Sourpuss.
'Let's do somefink really 'orrible,' said Billy Bogie, and spat into his own shadow.

Mrs Wobblebottom belched excitedly:
'I've got an idea! I've got an idea! Let's raid Farmer Giles's orchard and pinch some apples.'

All at once, everybody became very enthusiastic.

There were cries of:
'Great.'
'Good Idea.'
'What Naughty Fun.'
'Etcetera.'
King Pong quietened them all down.
'Hang on a minute, I've got an even better idea. Why don't we get hold of a few sawn-off shotguns and rob a bank?'
'Ooh, better still,' they all agreed, and set off immediately in search of a saw and some shotguns.

9 The Not So Great Bank Robbery – Part One

Luckily for everybody, the Stinkers couldn't find any shotguns, but they did manage to get hold of a saw. Billy B. knew a woodcutter who had accidentally sawn himself in two. So they called round to the house and borrowed it from his better half.

Now it was 2.30 p.m. and the mottled crew were all assembled outside Biggsy's Bank to spring the biggest, most daring, daylight robbery ever seen in the world, ever, for days.

King Pong volunteered to carry out the actual hold-up while the others kept his place in the bus queue. (There was no getaway car because none of them could drive, and they couldn't afford a taxi.)

Saw in hand, King Pong went straight up to the nearest cashier who greeted him with a cheerful:

'Good afternoon, Mr Pong, and what can I do for you?'

'This . . .'

'This is . . .'

'This is a . . .'

'This is a . . . This is a . . .'

(He could sense that something had gone horribly wrong – but what?)

'Stick-up. This is a stick-up.'

'Oh really Mr Pong, you are silly.'

'Your money or your wife . . . er, I mean life,' he persisted.

'If you want to be a proper bank robber,' explained the cashier helpfully, 'then you should wear a mask or a stocking over your head.'

King Pong blushed. Of course, that's what he had forgotten. He mumbled something about having left his camel parked on a double yellow line, turned and, getting the saw caught in his trouser turn-ups, stumbled, fell and crawled painfully out.

10   Some Useful Facts

The sole purpose of this chapter is to keep you in suspense as to what happens next in the bank.

As I believe that a good story should instruct as well as merely entertain, here are some facts that you may find useful . . .

1.   The third longest river in the world is the Yangtze in China. It measures 5,980 km from end to end.

2.   Mr Andy Clough of Knaresborough swallowed five live newts in seventy-five seconds to become the Yorkshire Live Newt Swallowing Champion. One of his opponents was disqualified for chewing.

3.   The largest lake in North America is Lake Superior, which is 83,270 km^2 all over.

4.   To prevent hot soup from spurting out of the can on opening, wait until it goes cold.

5.   If baby will not eat a banana, mash it into a pulp and add sugar.

6.   Liverpool is one of the largest and best-known cities in the area.

7.   The highest peak in Africa is Kilimanjaro which is 5,895 m high in its stockinged feet.

8.   The biggest chocolate éclair was made in Florida, USA. It was half-a-mile long, weighed 306 kg and contained over a hundred gallons of whipped cream.

9.   To remove chocolate stains from a white blouse or shirt, soak the garment overnight in red gloss paint.

10.   The world's most powerful pong is 4-hydroxy-3-methoxy-benzaldehyde. (The Stinkers like it on toast for breakfast.)

O.K. You can go now.

The nice helpful cashier (Marjorie Makeup was her name) was busily polishing an old 50p piece when someone demanded a billion pounds or else she would be sawn into kingdom come.

She looked at the saw waggling nervously in front of her and then at the face squeezed into one of Mrs Wobblebottom's nylon stockings.

'You remind me of a pound of sausages stuffed into a wine glass, or a waxwork figure starting to melt.'

'Stop messin' about. A million pounds and quick about it.'

Miss Makeup regiggled.

'A hundred pounds then. Fifty? O.K., I'll settle for a pound. 20p?'

'Look, Mr Pong, you really shouldn't waste the bank's time like this.'

'Mr Pong? I'm not Mr Pong. I'm Billy Bogie. Oops!'

'Well, Billy, you are silly. Even sillier than your silly friend. Fancy wearing a disguise and then introducing yourself.'

Ha Ha Ha

All the other cashiers joined in.

Ha Ha Ha

        Ho Ho

Billy Bogie blushed to the very roots of his boots, turned, and red, fled.

The Laughing Cashiers' Song

Ha Ha Ha
Ho Ho Ho
Off to the bank
Each day we go.

We don't sell haddock
Cod or trout.
Money is the thing
We care about.

We don't sell cabbage
Wheat or oats.
The only greens
We serve are notes.

Ha Ha Ha
Hee Hee Hee
A cashier's life
Is the life for me.

Safe behind
A wall of glass
We watch the rich
And poor all pass.

We cash their cheques
When in the mood
Or else say something
Really rude.

Counting money
All day long
Cashiers sing
A cashier's song

Ha Ha Ha
Hee Hee Hee
10 – 20 – 50p

Ha Ha Ha
Hee Hee Hee
A cashier's life
Is the life for me.

13   Unlucky for Some

Some people believe that thirteen is an unlucky number, although personally I don't. However, if you are superstitious, you are advised not to read this while:

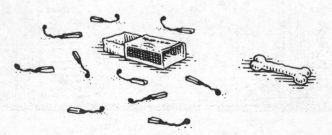

a. walking under a ladder
b. breaking a mirror
c. spilling salt
d. setting fire to a leopard
e. going over Niagara Falls in a barrel, wearing a suit of armour

14 Bank Holidays

As he strolled along the High Street, Emerson could hear the cashiers singing.

'They seem to be in a right good mood,' he thought. 'It must be a Bank holiday soon.'

Then his thoughts started giggling. 'Bank holiday? That's a funny idea. Fancy wanting to spend your holidays in a bank?' In his mind's eye he could see the adverts on television:

'This year why not take your holiday in a bank?...

A fortnight in Barclays, Blackpool, or a long weekend at the Nat. West. in Southend might be just the tonic.

Meet interesting tellers.

Witness the thrills and spills of accountancy.

And remember, you don't need a passport to spend the day at a foreign exchange counter.'

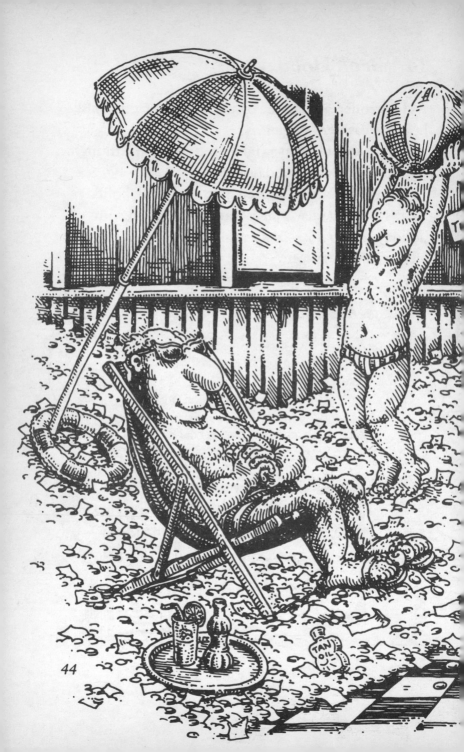

45

15　Fate Lends a Hand

Emerson was suddenly jolted out of his daydream by the sound of Billy Bogie, who came fullpelting towards him, hell for rubber.

'Good afternoon Billy,' called out Emerson in the cheeriest of voices. The Bogie blushed straight past without a word.

'Oh dear,' thought Emerson, 'it looks as if Billy got out of the wrong side of the spittoon this morning.'

On the pavement outside the bank he was surprised to find a saw and a warm nylon stocking.

'Odd,' he thought. 'Perhaps one of the customers dropped them. I'd better take them in and hand them over to one of the cashiers for safe keeping.'

16 *Fate Wants Its Hand Back*

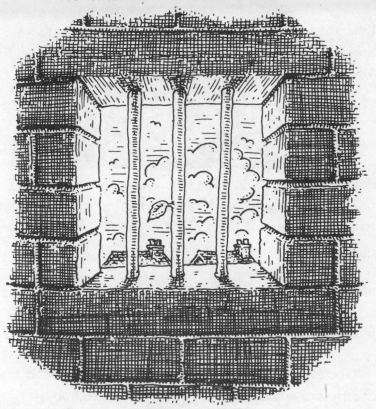

Emerson had never been in a prison cell before, and he didn't much care for it. Even his famous brave smile was beginning to wilt and fray at the ends.

It had all happened so quickly. One minute he was showing the saw and the nylon stocking to a laughing cashier and about to say:

'Excuse me, I found these on the pavement outside, do they perhaps belong to somebody hereabouts?'

And, before he could open his mouth, two burly policemen had grabbed him from behind with triumphant cries of . . .

'Gotcha!'

'Third time unlucky, mate'
and 'Thirty years for Bank Robbery'

. . . had hauled him outside and hurled him into the waiting Black Maria.

17 The Announcement

The long, winter months had been very hard for everybody, what with the bad weather and people out of work. And so the Government decided that the first day of spring would be a good time to cheer up the whole country.

So, on television that evening, the Minister for Happiness announced a competition to find the best smile in the land. Not enough people, he said, could be seen smiling in the streets. The nation seemed to have lost the art. Hence the competition. Whoever won would be given their own TV show so that every evening people could watch the famous smile and be happy.

Alone in his cell,

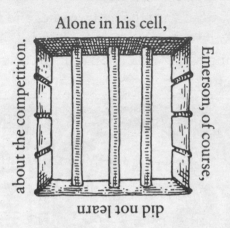

about the competition.

Emerson, of course,

did not learn

19 The 'Frown and Misery'

That night, the Stinkers were to be found in the backroom of their favourite pub, the 'Frown and Misery'. They were snarling at each other.

Spluttering, wheezing, coughing and cursing. They were dribbling down their fronts, burping and generally having a great time.

They had not been so cheerful earlier, though, after their embarrassing failure as bank robbers. But, having just watched the news of the smile competition on TV, they had quickly become their old stupid, greedy selves.

'Just fink,' said Billy, 'our own show on telly every night.'

'We'd be superstars,' said Nick O'Teen.

'Superstinkers,' said King Pong.

And they all raised their dirty glasses and drank to the success of The Superstinkers' Spectacular TV Show.

'Naturally, I'll be the biggest star of the show,' said Mrs Wobblebottom, eating a bag of crisps (without bothering to open it). 'I will be famous the whole world over for my radiant smile.' The others collapsed laughing.

'Radiant smile! That's a good one.'

'She's got a smile like a rusty letter-box.'

'. . . like a shark with tummy-ache.'

'. . . like an undertaker's false teeth in a glass of vinegar.'

'. . . like a cracked plate.'

'. . . like a loop of spaghetti dropped on the floor.' Mrs Wobblebottom wobbled furiously.

'You can all talk,' she screamed. 'You can all talk!' A fidgety hush settled over them like a fine grey dust.

'. . . like a fine grey dust,' said Sourpuss, always slow on the uptake. Mrs Wobblebottom turned on him:

'You, for example, you haven't smiled since you were a kitten. The last time you smiled was when your mother ran away. You've forgotten how to. And it's the same for the rest of you.'

'I've got a nice smile,' boasted Nick, halfheartedly.
'When something makes me smile, my face really
lights up.'

'The only thing that lights your face up is the match
at the end of a cigarette,' scoffed Mrs Wobblebottom.

The rest agreed. The sad truth dawned on them.
They never smiled, not one of them. They had all
forgotten how to.

'What we need,' said King Pong eventually, 'is a
nice pile of smiles to beg, borrow, or, better still, steal.
Any ideas?'

The silence of their thinking was interrupted only
by the steady munching of Mrs Wobblebottom as she
polished off her fourteenth snake and kidney pie.

Suddenly Billy Bogie removed a pool cue from his nostril and said:

'I've got an idea! Emerson, he's got heaps of smiles. He keeps them at home in a cupboard.' Everyone clapped their grubby hands and danced with joy.

'Good bad boy Billy,' they cried. 'Good bad boy.'

They quickly finished their drinks and, as they left the pub to carry out their evil deed, they sang the Stinkers' song:

We're the Stinkers, we stink
We're the Stinkers, we fink
We're the greatest, wink wink
We're the best at everyfink.

We like cobwebs and toejam
the underneath of stones
corners and shadows
bruises and bones.

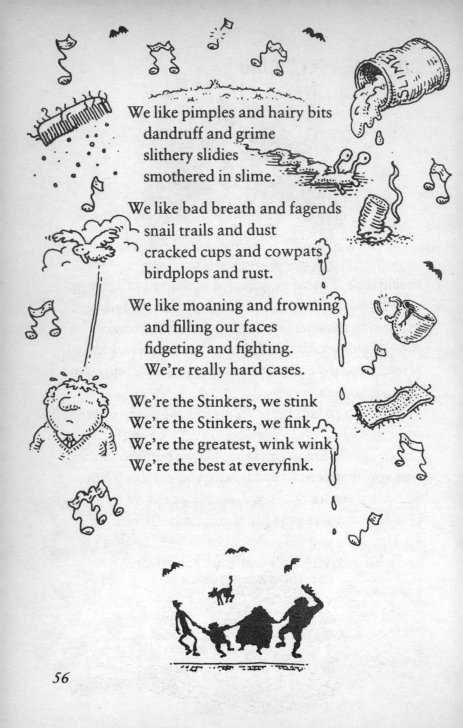

We like pimples and hairy bits
  dandruff and grime
  slithery slidies
  smothered in slime.

We like bad breath and fagends
  snail trails and dust
  cracked cups and cowpats
  birdplops and rust.

We like moaning and frowning
  and filling our faces
  fidgeting and fighting.
  We're really hard cases.

We're the Stinkers, we stink
We're the Stinkers, we fink
We're the greatest, wink wink
We're the best at everyfink.

Meanwhile, Emerson, feeling like this, was visited in his cell by P.C. Plod, an officer famed the length and breadth of the country for his kindness towards shop-snatchers, bag-pockets and pick-lifters. He had brought the lad a plate of biscuits and a steaming hot mug of cold tea.

'Err . . . well lad, there seems to have been . . . err . . . some mistake.' He explained, 'Err . . . wrongful arrest, I'm afraid . . . Err . . . but to . . . err is human, so I'm sure you'll understand. Anyway you eat this lot up and when you're ready give us a shout and I'll get one of the lads to give you a lift home in his panda car. And if I were you I'd go straight to bed 'cos you've had a busy day and it's well past your bedtime.'

Emerson thanked the kindly copper and then took
a biscuit for a paddle.

21 Ran Sacked

The Scene: A bedroom.
The Time: Later that night.

Emerson was fast, fast asleep and dreaming when the Stinkers, led by King Pong, tip-smelly-toed into the room.

Carefully avoiding the signs of snoring, they found the smiles cupboard

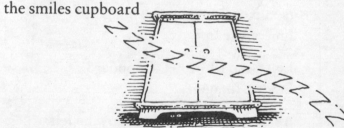

and ransacked it. Put all the smiles into a second-hand sack and ran. Ran, second-hand sack in hand.

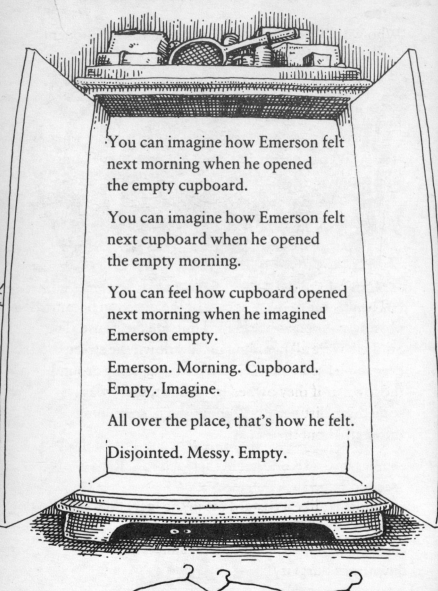

You can imagine how Emerson felt
next morning when he opened
the empty cupboard.

You can imagine how Emerson felt
next cupboard when he opened
the empty morning.

You can feel how cupboard opened
next morning when he imagined
Emerson empty.

Emerson. Morning. Cupboard.
Empty. Imagine.

All over the place, that's how he felt.

Disjointed. Messy. Empty.

23 The Page Shakes with Laughter

'Who would have done such an awful thing?' thought Emerson, 'and why?'

The answer to the first part of the question became obvious as soon as he stepped outside the house. The Stinkers were all parading up and down the street, ever so pleased with themselves. Swaggering around the town as if they owned it. And yet, there was something distinctly odd about them, something different about their faces.

Suddenly, like a custard pie in the face, the answer came to him! They were wearing his smiles. The cheek! The impertinence! What sauce! What downright burglary!

Emerson was so angry, his first reaction was to rush up to them and snatch the smiles off their silly faces. And then he realized that they were wearing them all wrong. The smiles were all over the place.

It was hilarious. Everybody in the street was laughing at them.

Emerson's eyes
Emerson's nose
Emerson's ears
Emerson's everything
Shook with laughter

Shook the whole page with laughter.

24 The Judges Judge

The page was still shaking with laughter when the people from the TV company arrived to judge the competition.

'Let's see who has the best smile in this street,' they said. 'Line up everybody and say: "Cheese".'

'Cheese,' roared King Pong
'Cheese,' sniffed Billy Bogie
'Cheese,' coughed Nick O'Teen
'Cheese,' hiccoughed Old Sourpuss
'Cheese,' burped Mrs Wobblebottom.

'Lots of smelly cheese around here,' said one judge.
'Very strange bunch of smiles indeed,' said another.
The third judge turned to Emerson:

'How about you son, will you give us a nice smile?'

Emerson wanted to more than anything else. To help cheer up people, to help them smile and feel happy.

'If only there was somebody out there who could help,' he thought.

'If only ....

.... If ....

.... only ....

.... If only ....

If .... only.'

....

....

....

....

....

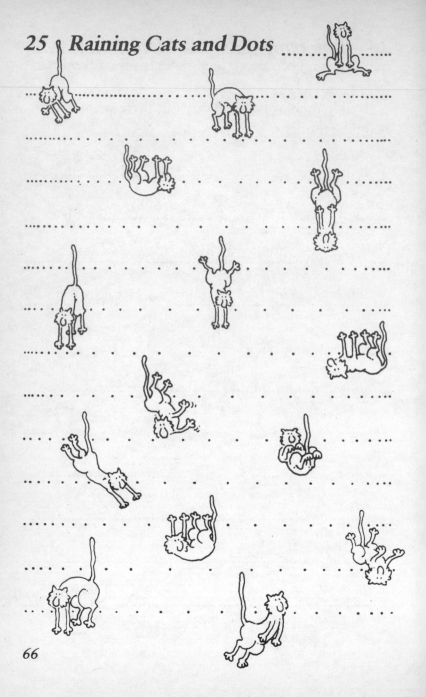

26 *Emerson Calls for Help*................

.... If only ....

Then he had an idea.

'If everybody in the world outside would smile at the same time, then maybe . . . just maybe, those smiles might shine through on to my face.'

Emerson looked straight at you and said:

'Smile please when I count three

One

Two

Three'

(Turn over the page and what do we see?)

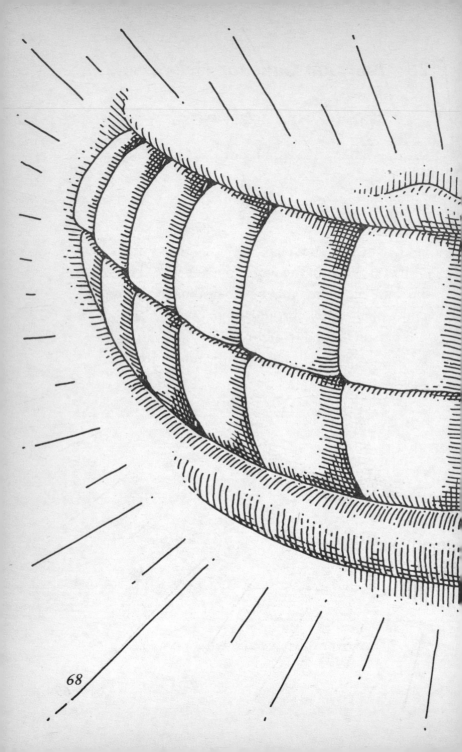

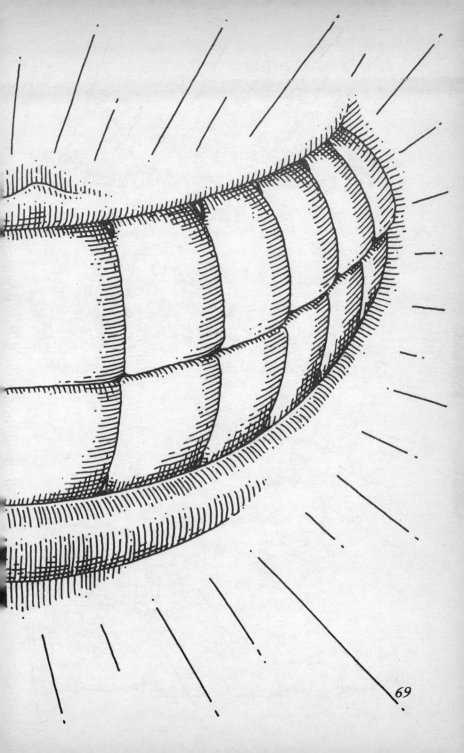

The judges were amazed. They'd never seen a smile like it.

'Stripe me pink,' said one judge.

'Tickle me with an elephant's feather,' said another.

'Winner by a mile,' said the third.

And without another word they lifted him high on to their shoulders and took him for a lap of honour around the town.

The people, how they cheered! And P.C. Plod, who was on point duty at the time, was delighted to hold up the traffic and let the happy procession cross the main road in safety.

'It's too, too wonderful,' he observed (putting too and too together).

28 *Launching Smiles into Outer Space*

So today, thanks to you, Emerson has his own TV show which is such a success that he travels all over the world teaching people how to make smiles.

There is even talk of him sending smiles into outer space. In fact, at this very moment he is in America discussing the idea with space experts there.

29 *All's Well that Ends*

And the Stinkers, what became of them?

Someone's insides caught fire in a drought
so the Fire Brigade couldn't put him out.
Who could that be?

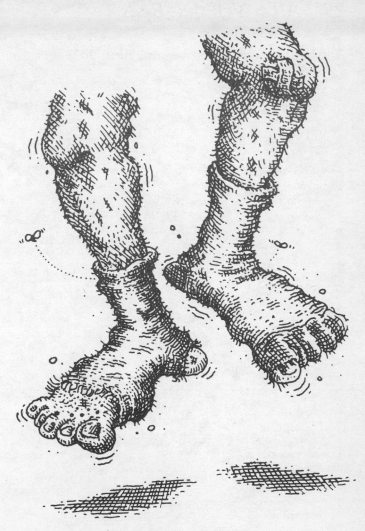

Someone's toes couldn't stand the smell
so they ran away (dirty knees as well).
Who could that be?

Someone, in winter, when everything froze,
got his finger stuck up his nose.
Who could that be?

Someone's botty one windy day
hobbled and bobbled and wobbled away.
Who could that be?

Someone caught fleas and gnats and nits
and scratched himself to little bits.
Who could that be?

30 YOU!

But the stinkiest Stinker
I ever did see
is the Stinker who's looking
straight at me.